Christmas Miracle

at

FIREHOUSE SEVEN

Thanks Mom, Juli, Brian, Bret, Meredith, Bob, and Anna

ISBN: 1461140862
ISBN-13: 9781461140863
Library of Congress Control Number: 2011907008
CreateSpace, North Charleston, SC

This story is dedicated to America's
Firefighters, Paramedics, and EMTs.
Especially those who were lost on September 11, 2001.

Merry Christmas! I hope you enjoy the story.

Jeff

Christmas Miracle
at
FIREHOUSE SEVEN

Jeff LeCompte

In the middle of town,
Was Firehouse Seven,
With an engine, an ambulance,
And Ladder Eleven.

The firefighters here
Were often quite busy,
With emergencies, fires,
Climbing ladders till dizzy!

But they all loved their jobs
At Firehouse Seven,
Jenny, Carlos, Jeff, and Evan,
Tony and Cathy on Ladder Eleven.

Jenny was smart.
She could think very fast.
When the others were puzzled,
They knew who to ask.

Carlos loved reading.
He had so many books.
And his firehouse friends,
Loved when he cooked!

Jeff often had
His eyes to the sky.
He loved climbing ladders,
Way, way up so high!

Cathy loved driving.
She did it so well.
The trucks were so big,
With sirens and bells!

And then there was Tony,
The firehouse clown.
He kept them all laughing,
With never a frown!

There was one big grump
At Firehouse Seven.
He seldom would smile.
His name was Evan.

He never said, "Thanks ,"
Or tried to be fair.
Some of the times,
He just didn't care.

But they made a great team,
Always helping each other.
They worked hard together,
Like sisters and brothers.

The seasons passed quickly
At Firehouse Seven,
With training and cleaning,
And complaining by Evan.

You see, Evan was angry
At a little grey mouse,
Who thought Firehouse Seven
Was his own cozy house.

The mouse often slept
In Evan's coat pocket.
When the fire bell rang,
He would scoot like a rocket!

While Tony just laughed,
And Jeff left mouse snacks,
Firefighter Evan ...
Searched for mouse tracks.

Well, winter arrived,
And snowflakes did fall.
And whoa! There goes Evan!
"Catch that mouse, down the hall!"

The mouse was afraid.
Evan didn't look nice!
So he squeezed past a door,
To the cold and the ice!

Evan stomped to the door,
And yelled at the mouse.
"Go away and keep out!
Find another mouse house!"

When the door was slammed shut,
The mouse cried sad tears,
Alone and afraid,
With Christmas so near.

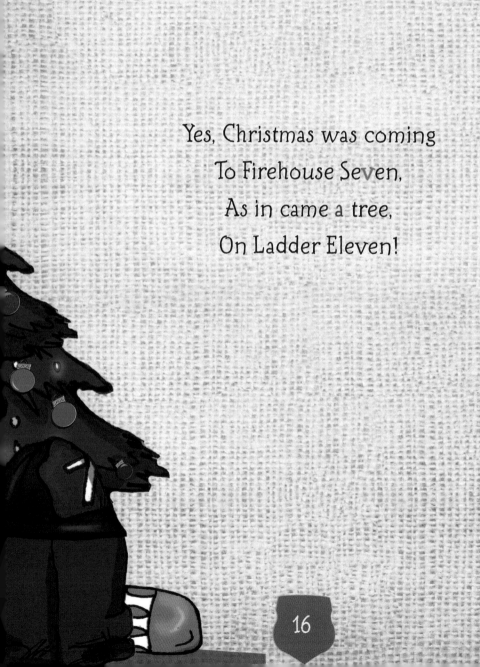

Yes, Christmas was coming
To Firehouse Seven,
As in came a tree,
On Ladder Eleven!

While Jenny and Carlos
Strung colorful lights,
One Christmas star
Was especially bright.

But Evan seemed quiet,
Decorating the tree.
Something was wrong.
What could it be?

Cathy and Tony
Tried cheering him up,
With steaming hot chocolate,
In a firehouse cup.

Evan said, "Nope."
And he seemed a bit sad.
Christmas was near,
And Evan felt bad.

TELL YOUR
MOM *and* DAD
to wear
SEATBELTS
because
YOU LOVE THEM

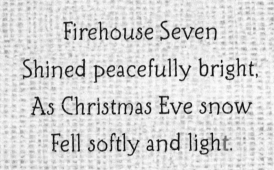

Firehouse Seven
Shined peacefully bright,
As Christmas Eve snow
Fell softly and light.

And holiday lights
Cast a colorful glow,
While the team in the station
Was ready to go.

All of a sudden,
The fire bell sounded!
Down the pole, to the trucks,
Their brave hearts were pounding!

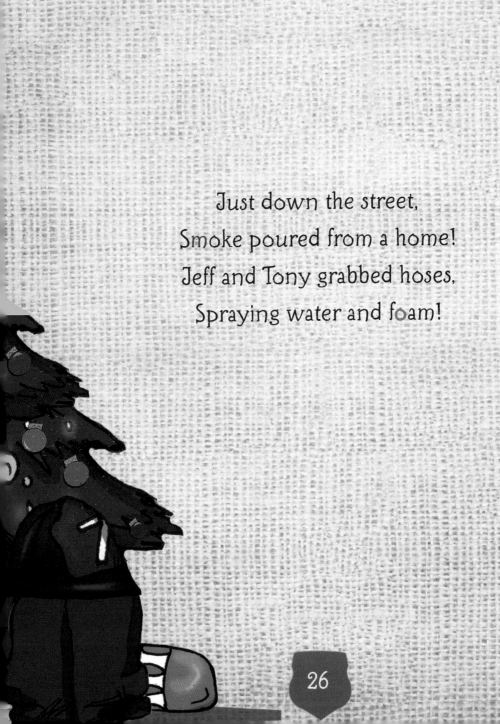

Just down the street,
Smoke poured from a home!
Jeff and Tony grabbed hoses,
Spraying water and foam!

Flames shot from the windows!
Orange glowed on the snow!
The big fire roared,
As more water flowed!

A neighbor yelled out,
"I don't think they're home!
Please do be careful!
Watch where you go!"

But deep in the smoke,
Evan searched through the home.
Checking room by room,
He sure felt alone.

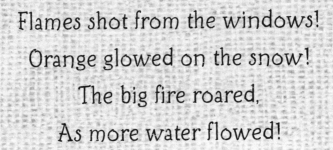

Outside, in the front,
Cathy set up a ladder.
Medic Jenny asked Carlos,
"Hey, what's the matter?"

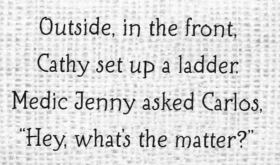

"The smoke is so thick,
That Evan got lost!
We must try to save him,
Through this fire and frost!"

Yes, deep in the home,
Evan tried to be brave.
But more and more smoke,
Made it dark like a cave!

But Evan's heart knew
He was lost in the smoke.
His strength was now fading,
And so was his hope.

Then a calm peaceful voice,
Told him, "Look to your right."
And there just beside him....
An astonishing sight!

The little grey mouse
He once chased away,
Was here by his side,
To show him the way.

Evan's eyes had glad tears,
As he crawled with the mouse,
Through the smoke, down the hall,
Outside of the house.

The little grey mouse
Was forgiving and brave.
He came to save Evan,
On this Christmas Day.

Partners Carlos and Jenny
Ran to his side!
So happy for Evan,
They smiled and they cried.

Then Tony came sliding,
Head first in the snow!
Jeff and Cathy hugged Evan,
Joyful hearts all aglow!

And deep in his heart,
Evan now knew,
He had to be kinder.
And he told them, "Thank you."

He hoped he could find
The little grey mouse,
Who forgave him and helped him
Escape from the house.

Some embers' soft hissing
Curled drifting steam.
But the house had been saved
By Seven's brave team.

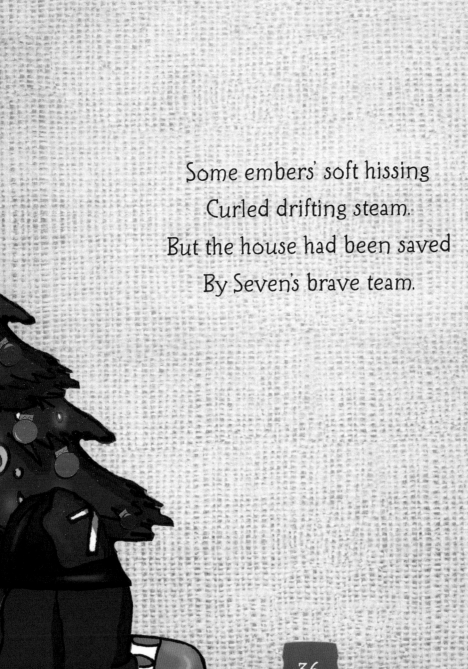

Back at the station,
The team cleaned their gear.
And the bright Christmas star
seemed nearer and nearer.

There was dry hose to pack
And ladders to clean.
But then something else
Caught the eye of the team.

They all stopped their work
And noticed a glow.
As the Christmas star's light
Beamed through the snow.

The light from the star
Shined on their coat rack.
The coat it made glow
Said, "Evan," on back.

The team was amazed,
And silently watched,
As the brave little mouse
Climbed in Evan's coat pocket!

Then they all hugged!
They high-fived and clapped,
So joyful to see,
Their mouse had come back!

His home now forever,
Was Firehouse Seven,
Safe and asleep,
In the pocket of Evan.

Merry Christmas from best friends, Evan and the mouse !

Merry Christmas from Firehouse Seven and America's Firefighters, Paramedics, and EMTs.

Made in the USA
Columbia, SC
26 September 2017